I Got Struck by 27 Thunderbolts: Love, Loss, and Lessons That Changed Me

From My Rain Of Thoughts

Published By Tony Storm

This book is a work of fiction, blending self-help, rom-com, and nostalgia-driven storytelling. While inspired by real-life scenes, exposures, emotions, and experiences, all characters, events, and dialogues are purely fictional. Any resemblance to actual people, persons, living or dead, is purely coincidental.

The lessons and insights shared in this book are based on personal interpretations and experiences. They are meant for reflection, inspiration, and entertainment, not as professional advice. Readers are encouraged to apply their own judgment and seek guidance from qualified professionals when making important life decisions.

The author is not responsible for any interpretations, feelings, or personal experiences that may relate to the content of this book. Any connections drawn are purely individual and unintentional.

Dedicating This Book To The People Who Made Me What I Am

To my Karmali Teacher, who taught me the real meaning of kindness—losing you felt like losing a piece of my soul.

To my Mother, who taught me to hold my head high, show up, and fight on even when failure looks bigger than Thanos and Godzilla.

To my Father, who shadowed me through all my big battles, unseen yet ever-present, I never noticed him, but I always felt he was just behind me, always.

To my Sister, who pushed me to read “The Alchemist”—a book that changed my life forever.

To my Pooja, my *Soulfate*, the rhythm of my heart in all its ups & downs, and the reason I still live.

To my sons, who flipped me inside out and shaped me into a better human—they pulled me far away from the mad Joker I once was.

To Sachin, who pulled me out from the depths of depression and suicidal thoughts, and who first inspired me to start writing this book and start a blog back in 2007.

To Chacko, who gave me the power, confidence, and vision to write this book—and every other non-fiction book that I have already written.

To Rahul, who taught me the real meaning of perseverance and to control my anger in unfortunate situations.

To Sanju, who taught me never to find pleasure in an enemy's failure.

To Deepak, my stress buster, who taught me the real art of being stress-free.

To Zeeshan, my inspiration to think big, dream big, act big, and achieve big in life.

To Arun, my inspiration to hustle life hard before life punches you in the face.

To Nirupama, who helped me understand what a girl truly expects from a boy.

To Rahul V, who reminds me to not have any sad thoughts in life—the one who always calls and asks, "*Da, nee happy alle*?"

To Joey, who taught me to find joy even in the greatest of all trials of my past GOAT life.

And finally, I am truly grateful to all 26 **thunderbolts** who rejected me, never said yes first, or never even gave me a chance to date them—you struck my life with **weird** and **unexpected colors**, shaping both my journey and the story I tell today.

I am Tony Storm, not *Tony Stark*

If you've ever felt like life keeps throwing thunderbolts at you—love, loss, heartbreak, failure, unexpected lessons—then we already have something in common.

I truly know what it's like to be shaped by the people around you, to be lifted up by some and broken down by others, to question everything and then find meaning in the chaos.

This book?

It's personal.

Every page has a flash of my memory and holds a piece of my journey, a collage of the stories of my friends, some scenes I felt like could have been better in life, some colors I saw others experience in front of my eyes, lessons from my teacher who showed me kindness, the words of my father who stood by me silently, the thoughts of my friends who pulled me back from the edge, and the ones who pushed me to chase something bigger.

And let's not forget the thunderbolts, rejections, the heartbreaks, and the people who walked away without even saying a single word.

They all left their scars, hope, and confusion, which somehow all led me here.

I started writing back in 2007, not because I had all the answers, but because I was searching for them.

And now, I'm sharing what I've realized—raw, unfiltered, and straight from the heart.

So if you've ever been struck by thunderbolts in life, if you've ever wondered why certain moments hurt so much but shape you so deeply—this book is for you.

And maybe, just maybe, you'll see a little bit of your own story in mine.

So thank you for picking up this book, for taking this journey with me, and for letting these words become a part of your story, too.

Writing this book was a journey—one filled with reflection, nostalgia, and a fair share of the colors of emotions I never expected to revisit.

But the fact that you're here, holding these pages, means everything to me.

It means these stories, these lessons, and these thunderbolts weren't just mine to carry—they were meant to be shared.

I hope that somewhere in these pages, you find a piece of yourself.

A moment that resonates, a lesson that speaks to you, or simply a reminder that no matter how many times life strikes thunderbolts, you're not alone in this storm.

From this moment on, you are officially part of my journey, just as I hope this book becomes a part of yours.

Table of Contents

Chapter Zero: Kick-Off, Life

She grabbed hard onto the bed.

It was getting worse; she had lost some fluid.

She was crushing her roots. Only she could be heard.

She cried out to her God an infinite number of times to bring him out safe.

She had asked him for this day and had a promise to keep. It was going to be real any time now.

She waited, but restlessness was in her veins.

She felt like an ice cube and a burning coal at the same time.

But still, she had a promise to keep, as she had asked for this day.

The clock wasn't ticking, the air wasn't known and the light wasn't seen.

Breakfast and lunch weren't heard for hours now.

And at 3:42 pm on a Wednesday her promise was received, her wish came true and hope was settled as she heard him kick-off to life.

This explosive couple gets blessed with an Aries star-studded baby boy.

The mother of this child had made a promise in the presence of God that she would name him after a saint, and so she did.

Terrance!

This boy was gifted like most other boys could have, special powers?

Naah, he was not a mutant nor from cyber-Tron.

But he was blessed, in a way that he could see through people, that is only if they wanted him to see through them.

Terrance was a really bad listener though.

Mostly the people whom he met especially women eternally had a soft corner for him only because of the fact that, he was amazingly artistic at solving their obstacles not just with a solution, but further with a plan in defeating their mayhem forever and helping them progress in life by slaying the pain.

He had a point:

"If you get everything you ask and wish for, then this place shouldn't be called *EARTH* but *HEAVEN*".

True right?

"I vouch on my stars on this - if you think you can then you can't, if you decide you can then maybe you could, but if you realize you can then should give it a full shot, you must jump to grab it”.

We often wait for opportunities, ask people for career advice.

But how many of us will dare to jump off that cliff and learn to fly as we fall?

Lol, well **Terrance** did it and is still doing it almost every day & hour after hour!

From My BLOG Verse 27:07

Year else-where and time no-where, **Terrance,** at the age of 5, collided with something called "emotions".

This realization struck him when he watched his mother—never just a homemaker, but an incredibly dedicated PhD Professor—effortlessly juggle a million tasks at once.

In just an hour, she would cook lunch, clean the house, bathe the kids, feed them, and still find time to correct her students' exam papers, all in a near-trance-like efficiency.

In this scene, **Terrance** experienced vibes in his body that he couldn't understand; he felt bad, broken, heavy, and his eyes moist.

He wanted to help his mother, but how much can a 5-year-old do.

He just couldn't do much.

Are all mothers the same, working their life off without expecting anything in return?

They do deserve more, after all this is the vicious circle of life. That very day Terrance decided and took a vow that happiness would be his priority, well not his happiness alone, but the happiness of the people around him at-least.

Moving ahead, the boy's childhood was otherwise fantastic.

Terrance lived in a city where there were no molesters around since life was more transparent then. He had at least 100 friends around.

He played gully cricket mostly and was a big fan of Mohd. Azharuddin and Ajay Jadeja.

He thought that this was the only outdoor game the world had.

It was the age when box TV was a trend and LED nor the internet was nowhere close in his vicinity. Those picked up late in the future.

One day Terrance decided to explore other sports channels, and thunder struck his brain for the first time in his life.

He saw the shortest guy among all the other 6-foot guys dunk a ball, bigger than a cricket ball into a ring with a net around it attached to a 10-foot post.

Damn, what was that?

For a split second, Terrance couldn't understand.

And then this guy on TV did it again, but this time jumping off from a real distance flying without wings.

Boom, that was Mr. Michael Jordan, the god of the game - basketball.

Terrance was in a wow mode.

How the heck did it do that?

Is this game in India?

His thoughts were all over the place.

There weren't many options to play basketball in those days except at school. So, he couldn't do much but get very little exposure to this game.

Terrance was heavily excited and figured out the whole truth that there was more to explore in this life.

School is a place to be if you want to figure out life.

The ecosystem there helps you to start to see the world from all angles. Hence every child must go to school, just ignore the YouTubers who say what can school actually teach you or they should have taught this at school.

So, choose a school that will allow you to figure life out and go to a school where there are kids from all walks of life, who can speak more than two languages. Else School is just another habit-forming tool for you.

Chapter One – Skipped a beat!

Why does a child cry on the first day at school?

I thought about it, asked people around, and researched a bit about it.

But still no answers, almost all are blank about this nor don't recall what happened to them on the first day at school.

Terrance was always curious, well most kids at the age of 5 are isn't it, or was he an exception here too?

Class three at school, that’s how we refer to 3rd Grade at school in India.

At the edge of a rainy season, the sky was mostly the color of charcoal, but the air was crystal clear and cool, a bit windy though, there were a few birds trying to get back to their nests, squirrels running around in joy.

And most importantly a big group of 3rd-grade kids, girls & boys were playing the game of catch me if you can - the robber & police game.

In this game, the girls were always the police and as always, the boys' robbers.

As I write this, it really struck me that, kids of this age group are quite funny and very innocent.

The only thing that we lost growing up is innocence.

In the pursuit of happiness, the first thing that we lose is innocence, the rest all follow!

And this is one sacrifice that you will have to make in life as you evolve.

I know for a fact that the price I paid for my growth and hustle in a decade-plus of my career is innocence.

That’s the only thing that I have sacrificed in my life to date and I know for a fact that it will never come back to me, it’s gone forever.

I can never be that innocent child again in this storm!

Back to the story –

The rule of the game 'Catch Me If You Can' was that the girls had to catch all the boys including their "leader" – the main "robber" to win the game. And the boys could only win the game if they were all not caught till the school bell rang.

So, the game kick-started in full swing, boys were running like crazy zebras and the girls were like cheetahs.

It was truly a race out there fast n furious style!

Between all this confusion, **Terrance** who was the leader of the boys in this game was tired of running and took a tiny break to catch some air, he hid behind a big banyan tree, and looked at the clouds, "seems like it's gonna rain".

And boom!

He felt like some small weight fell on him.

Aah no, darn guess he got caught!

He fought to find a clear vision and was trying to figure out what was happening.

And it happened as it had never happened before, he felt shaken and numb, his heartbeat was falling slowly, unsure if it even skipped a beat, palms sweaty and heavy.

The background of his vision was pitch black and he could only see a girl holding his collar and standing just close to him.

In a flash, the image of this girl looked just like a pink cute cuddly teddy bear, gosh!

Damn, what the heck was happening!

The boy in third grade at school couldn't figure out what was wrong with him, "was it a thunderbolt", did he get hit by lightning or was it a panic attack?

He just looked frozen, perplexed, and tongue-tied.

To this, the girl yelled out loud saying "Caught the leader, end of the game".

It started to rain, as heavily as ever.

Terrance didn't know what to say he could only still see her vaguely through the big droplets. Unusually these raindrops were as big as a toffee.

Other than the girl everything around Terrance was pitch dark and jet-black.

"Tring Ring Ding Tring Ring Ding" roared the school bell and that was the end of the day at school.

Terrance was just flowing on the ground like Michael Jackson, he couldn't feel like he was walking.

Suddenly his friends rounded him and started yelling - "Hey, hey, yo man".

Are you ok?

What happened to you all okay?

You seemed to be so pale with zero expression!

Terrance could barely speak; he felt like all those words were too heavy to spill out.

But his friends forced him to narrate the entire game scene and now everyone around him also looked confused and tongue-tied too.

He couldn't still understand what happened to him and why his body reacted to that girl in such a way.

He was a bit scared and wanted reassurance of what had happened.

So he decided to approach his much intelligent lookalike elder sister for some advice.

As usual, since they weren't the best of friends or foes he was sure that there could be some progress to his incident.

He went straight home where he belonged and waited for his sister to reach home.

As always Terrance had a starting problem with the presentation.

He thought “How can I trust her (*sister*), what if she tells my parents?

Well seems like this is it, there is no other way to know this, really can’t go back and ask his teacher though!

Now she (*sister*) came in, and **Terrance** was ready with the presentation.

So, the best way to present this could be to offer her some tasty lip-smacking and finger-licking mom made hot banana fritters (*Kerala style*) snack, that Terrance had saved for her, he thought.

Well, he did just that.

Always remember you have to get a lady’s full attention, her permission, and her clear mind first before speaking anything important to her. This is one of the best ways to get the correct answer to any question and a truly open view on any subject.

So he did just that, he narrated the entire scene the same way I have written above and it happened.

The final verdict from a very intelligent elder sister any boy would be blessed to have. Well maybe!

She (*sister*) said in a very polite but excited tone “Yo fool, it's LOVE, I think you are in LOVE dude, for the very first time!”

Terrance - Love, huh, yikes what’s that, is it a disease am I gonna die, will a doctor help, should I tell Mom, how can I get over it?

Sister: You can’t bro, because you are not under it, it is inside you, it is an expression, a deep complex emotion, or can even be called an action by which any rock statue melts, you will figure it out better by yourself tomorrow at school and she left him drowning in his thoughts.

By then **Terrance** understood two new things in life. One - a piece of new music called “LOVE” sounds like jazz to him and, Two - basically sisters’ are not that great at solving stuff. But they are quite good at making you think and do a job; well that’s how life lessons should be.

So, what is </**LOVE**> to you?

Chapter Two – Cowabunga To Friendship

Terrance was confused, couldn't understand a thing, and was really mind-stuck after listening to his sister's titanic story about "love".

He was still curious to know what was gonna happen next.

He also thought if he should tell his parents about this.

And that's when, in the middle of all this story it was raining "love" outside.

Yes, it was still raining heavily.

Well if you have been to Kerala, it still feels like love is in the air when it rains. That's how you feel when you experience rain in this land, there will be a fresh charming smell of red mud, the drumming sound of thunder, a pitch charcoal dark background with lightning-like camera flashes, and if you have a red umbrella plus a girl next to you, it would be a perfect frame finish for a love scene in Shah Rukh Khan's next movie.

But I am sure a third-grade schoolboy wouldn't have felt the same way I have just narrated rain here.

Terrance was haunted by this feeling, so he decided to tell the girl tomorrow at school.

He was curious to know if she also felt the same.

He slept well that night, which normally doesn't happen in other love stories, hmm?

In his normal routine, he got up in the morning and ate the nutritious large breakfast that his mom made with her magical palms.

God, mothers are still the best cooks in the world, they know what you should eat for breakfast.

Missing my mom's morning tea right now while writing this. That tea was like a high electric energy drink.

The boy was unusually 7 mins earlier to school than his usual arrival time.

He went right to his classroom and greeted the empty desks.

It was a Friday and none of his buddies had arrived.

For a minute he forgot about the girl while he looked around at his beautiful classroom.

Wow, was an understatement, the classroom was looking very alive. It had a lot of beautiful pictures hanging around, and that's when he realized that it's been 7 months in this class and he hadn't ever checked out a single picture.

Why?

How did he miss this?

A busy schedule in life can push you to look in one direction only at times. It's best to look around when you are stuck in traffic rather than honking hard to move on. Pause at a time to Shuffle life ahead!

Terrance then stood up and took a stroll inside the classroom; while browsing through all those pictures, he came across a crayon drawing. It had a black horse and a red warrior with a sword standing next to it in a brown dry desert.

What type of drawing was this and who drew it?

It had no name nor a signature, and what was the drawing all about, was this warrior lost?

Then a bell rang, and he realized that he had been staring at that picture for some time now and that his buddies had reached the classroom and were getting ready for the morning school assembly.

The morning assembly was the best positive way to start off school those days; which was later set as a strategy by the big MNCs, but ended as a not-so-positive morning assembly or huddle for the employees. This later failed in 2020, when they figured out that, these not-so-positive early meetings before the start of work decreased productivity drastically as the team leaders and bosses didn't have the required positive energy or skills in them to motivate their employees to kick start their day's monotonous routine.

Terrance browsed the entire class, but couldn't find the girl.

So he checked for her at the assembly.

Being short she was at the start of the line where the kids stood in height order (*from shortest in the front to the tallest at the back*) for the school assembly.

Terrance thought that she might be late, so he waited restlessly till the school assembly was over. And rushed back to class before the teacher arrived, but to be disappointed again to find that the girl wasn't there either.

Suddenly their teacher came into the classroom.

The kids wished her with the boring “*Namaste teacher*” song.

Terrance was still unknowingly waiting to see her even after the teacher marked her attendance as absent for the day.

He was a bit sad, only a bit sad today.

That day he didn’t talk much to his friends, as for him it ended the way any sad movie could.

There was obviously another day coming.

Waiting for someone is an unexplained feeling, it is a color blend of sadness and happiness, and it doesn't have a definite end.

Unless and until time stops, it keeps ticking to that moment which decides everything, and once the wait is over, you realize that one of these colors was real, so it's good to be color blind.

Terrance was only a bit sad since he had the weapon of hope and the shield of time in hand.

The next day also ended the same way as the other day and also the days that came after it.

Seven days passed by, and now Terrance was anxious, angry and wanted to know what happened to the girl.

All these days he waited for her and didn't have the guts to go around and ask people.

But today was not that day, he went up to one of the boys who used to sit behind her, and there were other few boys around him.

And they were discussing hard about something.

Since their conversation was of high energy and exciting, **Terrance** gave an ear to it.

Those boys were saying *Cowabunga* dude at times.

Wow, that was cool to hear, well what does that mean? He then asked them.

Everyone laughed out loud and booed, and one of the kids even yelled out - Don't you even know that, how come, which part of the earth are you from?

Terrance was stunned; how come he didn't know it when the entire class was bragging about it?

The entire class laughed at him again, and this made him badly upset. He even forgot about the girl and even forgot to ask that boy about her in all this confusion.

That day after school, before boarding the school bus, he saw that boy again and rushed up to him.

God, he was again with other boys this time too.

But our boy didn't hesitate to ask him this time.

Before he could open his mouth and throw out that question. A boy stopped him.

Jayce - Well well well, look who is here to ask us the meaning of *Cowabunga.*

Terrance – Hey, I don't want to know that, but I want to know where that girl is.

Kids, right, they like playing games all the time!

Jayce – Who?

Terrance - That girl you know!

Jayce - Which girl, dude?

Terrance - That girl who caught me the other day in the catch game!

Jayce - Wait, what, you don't know her name. She is our classmate and has been with us for three years now.

Terrance - What really, I don't know, I haven't noticed her, I got transferred from another class - remember dum dum!

Jayce - This is so you, a bad listener. So, you really don't know her name, do you?

Terrance - No bro, I don't. But I need to know, please!

Jayce - Alright chill, I will tell you that but you have to tell us the meaning of *Cowabunga* by tomorrow.

Terrance – Why should I, moreover I don't know it.

Jayce - Well that's the game stupid, I will give you a clue, find that and I will tell you where she is.

Terrance - Ok, deal then, shoot me with the clue.

Jayce - Watch this show at 7 o'clock today on Cartoon Network and that's your clue.

Terrance - Huh, alright, whatever, but you better be ready with my answer tomorrow.

Oh god, kids can at times be very challenging in some situations, phew!

And the wait was on for the 7 o'clock show, but then Terrance felt a mix of yellow and gray, was he nervous again?

Unlike recent times, back in those days there were hardly 10-15 TV channels in India and only one prime news the Fathers watched daily and that always happened right at 7 pm, this was a problem for our boy.

But the best part slipped in when his mom told him that, Dad was coming home very late that night.

Phew, problem one solved.

Now comes problem number two, his sister wanted to watch the “Hit Me Baby One More Time” song on MTV at the very same time.

Have you ever noticed this at work or in life?

Wherever you want something very important happening - a deadline or a date time that you are chasing?

You will feel like there are trillions of things and people trying to stop you from achieving it. There will be another million obstacles, but if you stop at just one with at least a 1% self doubt - you are busted!

Well as always, the last resort for Terrance was an all-purpose emotional line “Mom, this is the last time I will ask you for it, next time I won’t”, to this any mother in the world will help you. I swear.

But this time Terrance told her as part of a new school project he wanted to watch Cartoon Network for 27 minutes at 7 o’clock.

Do you really buy that, the boy’s mother was sure that it was a lie and he was up to something.

But wanted to find out, hence gave him a chance.

Lol, his sister was really pissed!

The clock did an unusually slow walk up to 7 PM, breaking its normal fly-to time.

That night was slow, well that's what happens when you wait, you are always ahead in time and time walks behind you. You feel like the world has taken a pause and staring at you for no reason. And feel like everyone is interested in what you are trying to do in life.

At times clock stops when you want something immediately - good things in life should take some time, or else you will forget it fast!

And then the show started off with a song "Teenage Mutant Ninja Turtles, (*repeating a couple of times*), darn what was this?

Was **Jayce** fooling **Terrance**, was it a joke?

But **Terrance** decided to patiently watch the show.

This cartoon had four turtles, one rat, and one cruel-looking samurai warrior in an iron suit.

Whoosh, ninja stunts all over, the storyline was interesting the four turtles and the rat were mutated in some green fluorescent stuff and they grew up to be human-like (*standing on two legs*) and doing martial arts - ninja style.

Wow, the cartoon was too good; **Terrance** felt happy and was thanking **Jayce** in his head for this new exciting thing he had shared.

But wait, what the heck is *Cowabunga* and why was he watching this cartoon for that; **Terrance** couldn't understand a thing.

Again, in those days, most shows were for 30 minutes wherein 27 minutes was for the story play and 3 minutes for advertisements. Unlike these days for a 30-minute show, the story play was for 10 minutes and 20 minutes was for paid advertisements, right?

Back to the screen, the show ended, but with the credits rolling down and at the fag end of it a turtle with an orange eye tie came up to the screen and said "*Cowabunga dude*".

Hearing this, **Terrance** was jumping with joy and he was so proud that he was able to figure this out finally.

At times you wait, hope, wait, expect, wait, think about, wait, wish, wait, and finally when it happens and realize that the wait is over, it happened and the wait is over - do you feel happy because the wait is over or because you achieved it?

When the wait is over, I normally feel happy because of the fact that I achieved it and sad because of the fact that the happiness that I experienced while waiting is finally over.

So, now the wait was for the next day for school.

“The feeling of finding something after waiting or searching for it, is still unknown, as for a second after this, it could make you happy or sad at the fact that it is now over, the wait or search is over and done with forever”.

Terrance reached the school the next day, this time, not early but late, he then looked around a bit for that Girl, darn she wasn’t there still, instead found **Jayce**, gosh at least he was there, and this time alone.

Terrance caught up to the **Jayce** straight, told him about *Cowabunga* which was a lingo used in TMNT and had nothing in meaning.

Jayce - Welcome (*thrilled*) to the gang buddy!

Now it was his turn to tell **Terrance** where the girl was.

Terrance asked him again “Buddy tell me what the hell happened to her”.

Jayce - Dude her name is **Lilly,** at least stop saying girl from now!

Wow, what a beautiful name for a pink teddy bear-like girl, **Terrance** was in a trance.

He came out of himself just like Hulk did in the Avengers movie scene with the Ancient One!

And then, **Jayce** brought him back to reality when he said "Bro, she left our school a week back, didn't you know?"

Terrance was instantly red, muted blue, dark orange, deep red all colors of *crushed, upset, angry, furious, and sadness* were over him, but didn't cry yet.

He then ran away pushing **Jayce** aside saying – "what friend are you, you made me do all this to hear this at the end".

Jayce couldn't understand what was happening but was also feeling sad at the fact that he just made and lost a new friend in a split second.

Understand and note this please, "when you are angry the best thing to do is to just, first, leave the damn place you are standing at, because at that moment nothing works as your body would start doping itself with specific stress hormones or chemicals that blocks your brain and heart connection first, and then next it ensures that your boneless tongue starts talking unwanted phrases and hands start raising undesirable actions".

It's seriously true and happens to me all the time!

Terrance needed time, the time to sink into this scene, accept the fact that boom, **Lilly** was gone forever and he was hurt because he couldn't tell her that, he...

The scene here was for him to accept the truth with an incomplete action, it was tough.

When you miss that bus, when you miss that opportunity, when you miss that deal - it hurts.

But it's more painful and regretful when you miss telling someone who matters most to you in the world, what you feel for that person, and when you know that things will not be the same ever again!

The next day school for **Terrance** was looking different.

So different in a way that the classroom, teachers, classmates, the building, the ground, the school bus, and his uniform were all the same, but the bench in the classroom that **Lilly** sat was empty and that was the difference, the difference only he saw.

But thankfully knew for sure that she was not coming back tomorrow.

His hope ends here!

They always say in tough times do not worry - God is looking at you from the top.

Well, I just want to add something more:

Not just God is looking at you from the top, what about other directions around you?

Why do you only look above, there are also others looking at you from all directions.

Your friends,

Your family,

And especially your teacher is checking if you are daydreaming in class.

So was **Jayce**, he could understand that **Terrance** was unsettled here and wanted help.

And wasn't confident if he could speak to our boy after the latest incident between them. But for sure wanted to try, so he went up to their math teacher; and requested if he could sit next to **Terrance** in her class as he had a short-sight problem with his eyes and couldn't see the black math board from the distance where he was previously sitting.

The teacher did the right thing by allowing **Jayce** to sit next to **Terrance**.

A couple of days went by and **Terrance**'s ego blocked him from listening or speaking to **Jayce**.

This can't go on for a year, how long would I not speak to him, the year at school is gonna end in a few weeks from now. **Terrance** though.

Terrance was not bad at heart and always had a spike in curiosity, one day he decided to kill the *"E"* in his EGO and to this, *"GO"* ran away.

Then at school one day it finally happened!

Terrance told **Jayce** what he went through and how he felt about **Lilly**, his thunderbolt of love, and everything.

Great now **Jayce** just like **Terrance** couldn't understand a thing, he was also confused.

But then came up with an idea, he told **Terrance** to speak to **Lilly** from a landline phone.

Wow, this is why a "*friend in need, is really a friend indeed*".

Jayce – Bro why don't you give her a call?

Terrance - How, I don't have **Lilly**'s number.

Jayce – What are you saying, the school telephone index was given to all our parents and it will have her home phone number for sure.

Terrance - Is it, oh yes I have seen my sister using it, huh, would she have called someone she loved? Has she used it for the same purpose that I want to?

Jayce – So what, your goal is to call **Lilly**, right? Just focus on that dude.

Terrance – Yeah true, well thanks buddy, and; and am really sorry about what happened that day. Are we friends, now?

Jayce – That we already are buddy, see you at school next week, all the best with the call.

Back to **Terrance**'s sister at home!

He went straight to her room and asked her for the school telephone book.

Sister - Why do you need it, kiddo?

Terrance - Uh, I want to call an old friend.

Sister - That's a bit odd! Here, take it.

On getting the telephone book, **Terrance** searched the whole book like *Liam Neeson* in the movie *Taken*. He almost ripped a few pages.

Yessssssssss, found it!

Next he waited for the right time, you see in those days the land phone was always kept next to the TV in the living room. And damn that is where the entire family was almost chilling around. There was no privacy if you spoke to someone on the phone, the entire neighborhood would know soon.

Terrance waited there like the sniper in that web series '*The Day of The Jackal*'.

Finally, after a long 4 hours, the coast was clear now, and he did it, he dialed **Lilly**'s number.

"Trinnnngggg Trrrrinnggggg", kept ringing for a couple of seconds and then an AI kinda voice answered the phone.

Terrance was suddenly thrilled to only understand that it was an auto-recorded "no answer" regret call message on the landline by BSNL.

Hmm, who was that, still she had a very sweet voice though.

He was disappointed as this ended really fast unlike a scene in any suspense thriller movie.

But **Terrance** didn't give up, he went back to his sister and told her that the number mentioned there was wrong.

She then told him that the book was a year old and the latest one hadn't been published yet.

Damn, **Terrance** lost hope here in a jiffy.

Seeing his expression change, his sister gave him another hope to check the "Yellow Pages", it was a public telephone directory.

Dang, who said sisters aren't sensible, well his was!

Terrance did just that, he checked the yellow book, searched like a Marco trooper, and found it there it was in black printed-on-white telephone numbers of his **Lilly**, which was to his eyes written in gold.

He picked up the landline telephone and rang that number.

Hope tringgging this time and after a couple of rings the same sweet voice answered the phone again, that was the same auto-recorded “no answer” regret call message from BSNL.

Terrance was deeply hurt and depressed.

Did you know that a couple of seconds before the start of a depression, our emotions get neutralized by a wave of sadness, and emptiness, the body becomes numb at various places, and a sense of mental fog creeps in, making it hard to think clearly and then the eyes get filled up with a slow gloomy sea.

This was almost happening to **Terrance** as well.

But remember, since he was an Aries star-studded fiery ram at heart, he wheeled the scene like in the *Inception* movie and just flipped the picture, which then started rolling backward.

That is when he realized that God was watching over him all this while, also in the form of a “best friend”.

Terrance realized that he got here because of **Jayce** who in the first place told him the bad news (*reality*) and then helped him with the solution to it.

When all tricks in life fail, friends appear from heaven to teach you the real trick!

So, the wait is now on to meet **Lilly** someday and tell her what **Terrance** couldn't say then, will that happen?

Let's see as this globe is a small loop and time is short, hence they should meet someday for sure.

From all this **Terrance** figured out that the solution to all his problems always ends up with another problem.

So his problems were never really a problem, but their solution was the biggest problem.

The solution to his problems was always there at the beginning of all his problems, only the time taken and the journey to find the solution was the actual problem.

Now while writing this I just realized that; friends happen for a reason, they teach you a lesson, they help build your life story with theirs, they push you to unimaginable limits, they kick your ass when you are wrong, they stand invisibly strong behind you even without you noticing them, while you need them bad and most frankly; a friend who picks you up in their journey will ride miles ahead with you in life.

Well, ain't I blessed, am a rider myself!

So, you still </**Waiting**> for that someone?

Chapter Three – Rebound, like a basketball

Terrance had lost an emotion, but couldn't figure out why.

He suddenly felt a gap in his life.

What the heck was it?

God to resolve.

In life, you will gain something when you lose something; if you say No to pain, then it's a No to Gain as well, and this is what I have figured out.

To get new friends, you will have to let go of some, hence be careful about what you wish for at times, (*haha*) only at times.

Then why do you have to do this when you know that you will lose some?

The truth is that it's all in the situation one is in, whether bad or sometimes too good to remember the happiness it had.

Hence you cannot blame anyone for this.

Now when a good friend stops calling you suddenly without any reason, just understand that he or she needs help and who else can help him or her better than you.

So why wait again for their call, just pick up the phone and call them, right now!

His days ahead at school were quite blank unlike before.

The same old story was happening again and again in black and white.

The sense of not seeing **Lilly** was killing his story.

He wanted only a minute with her, just to tell her what he felt, just to tell her what he had experienced and just to know if she felt the same.

But the *yellow* truth was that he couldn't, as she was no more at school, she was gone, she went off like a tornado, destroying his moment and leaving him broken behind with her in his thoughts.

She is now in his history of some unsolved mysteries that he will have to keep to the grave.

But still, **Terrance** had a depression-proof jacket on him, which could be the prayers of his mother or because of his friends around.

He had some good friends around him, boys with sound values and morals.

At that age of innocence, it's too true to go wrong.

The boys always kept him active, how?

They played cricket, and that was the most played outdoor game in India in those days.

This kept him occupied, slowly in the rush to hit a six and make a century he almost forgot about **Lilly**.

To recover from a fall, jump higher; to shoo away breakup and depression take a deep nap and make a rebound, it's not easy, try it to buy it later here.

Rebound - it reminds me of my basketball game times at college.

A rebound is the best way to score when you are blocked by more than one opponent.

For **Terrance** the the game was **Lilly**; the opponents were his thoughts about her who was blocking him from scoring in life, and he wanted a rebound to just score again, forget the past and win.

And then one day in the game called life, **Terrance** passed the ball to a friend who passed it to a Girl who threw a rebound. **Terrance** took the rebound and scored a three-pointer basket right there!

Neenu was dusky, with dark mocha brown lips, skinny for her age, black short hair, and had the nerve of a cat, bit short-tempered though.

She was one year older than **Terrance**.

That day, his scene changed from black and white to a colour frame.

This time not skipping a beat, but it felt like being hit by a “Thunderbolt" again.

Damn, what was it again?

What was that feeling?

Why is the background turning pitch charcoal black again, not that god, not that again!

Terrance could only relate the present scene with the scene he experienced with **Lilly**.

This time, he was cautious but with curiosity; he didn't want another pathway to the overwhelming verge of a depressed state.

He saw **Neenu** at the color-lit festival of his parish church, that was a real treat for sad eyes.

The lighting around looks even better than the Eiffel Tower, the best part was the small shacks lit up with flickering little kerosene lamps.

It had everything a kid could probably wonder about, right from small simple toys to cotton candies.

Neenu wasn't cuter nor was she looking like a pink teddy bear.

But was definitely a rebound, it was, it really was a rebound for **Terrance**.

Well, he couldn't figure that out yet.
He glanced at her a couple of times, but like all girls, she was extremely busy shopping and gazing into those shacks with the huge crowd around.

Mostly at times I get really worked up and cautious if am with a girl in any huge crowd.

Nowadays anything can happen, but those days were much safer and one mostly din’t have to worry about pick-pockets.

And now in recent times...

It's almost every man's nightmare and sometimes the lady's too.

Terrance was looking forward to talking to **Neenu** someday, but something in his gut told him that he is going to meet her in 1,2,3 and boom the moment, their families knew each other (*as in any Bollywood movie*).

Well, that was a coincidence in disguise for the boy. The boy wanted to say a “hello" to her, but no chance she was too busy with shopping, the typical girl he thought.

He then turned back and even saw his sister & mother were busy shopping too.

He thought “why do these girls shop a lot and keep buying, no wonder these shacks were open till midnight until the girls were off to sleep, I guess they even shop in their dreams, oh gosh!"

Terrance then tried to get **Neenu**’s attention with a small hand wave.

Okay, well that didn't work, she was too busy to notice.

He then did something that should never be done to a girl.

Kids right, little he knew.
He gave her a small kick on her leg, and slash was the sound he heard.

He heard a sound like a sword swing, ouch, he got a hit on his shoulder blade.

And it felt like a bee sting, **Terrance** thought that he fell off the ground, but figured out with his leftover consciousness that the girl had hit him back really hard.

What the heck was that, was she a ninja or a *Karate Kid*?

Girls at times can hit you back badly, so don't play silly with them!

Terrance was stunned at this, the funny part was that lucky for him **Neenu** did not yell out nor scream, phew!

Otherwise, the scene could have been terrible.

But that was weird, she didn't say anything, one wack and that's it.

Okay, this is going to be interesting, **Terrance** thought.

So he didn't make another move to get her attention as the day was already full of what he had just received.

Terrance's thoughts were full again with questions yet empty for more!

How could **Neenu** not notice him even after that incident or was she acting as if she hadn't seen him or was she purposely ignoring him or has she felt the same way he just felt for her, or is she blind, oh god?

So, ever got a ≤**thunder bolt**≥ or a </**rebound**>?

Chapter Four – A Kiss Of Confusion

Terrance was watching an action movie in English at home, the scene was a hostage situation, there was a bomb hidden in a running bus.

Like all action heroes, this guy in the scene was trying to save the hostages, but the movie didn't have the villain also in the bus unlike the normal Bollywood movies, which was a bit confusing.

Well, the suspense went on and on, and on until it reached a scene before the credits rolled, and it happened again **Terrance** was stunned, surprised, confused, god what was that?

The hero did something that spiked loads of suspense in him.

The hero went up to a lady and did something that **Terrance** couldn't understand.

What was that again, it just happened in a dash, it felt intense and intended to be an expression of something that **Terrance** couldn't figure out.

That image was clicked and stored in his brain.

Terrance was restless now, he wanted to tell someone about what he witnessed on TV.

But to whom can he ask, obviously not his sister - no way!

Nor to his mother - are you serious!

Then comes the best option in anybody's life – friends. Great, he did just that.

The next day at school **Terrance** was feeling a bit shy but still thought, why should I be shy to my friends?

I can say, ask, and share anything in this world with them, so what are friends for?

Well, this is why they are here!

So he decided to go to the most experienced friend of his - **Jayce**.

There was a reason why **Jayce** was the most experienced friend in his circle, well he was a year older than the rest of the boys.

Don't ask how a guess would be better. So **Terrance** went up to him –

Our Boy: Hey, wassup?

Jayce: So, tell me what is it?

Terrance: Shocked! Damn, how did you know that I had something to tell you?

Jayce: (*Chuckles*) "That's experience bro", it's written all over your face.

At times even I get stunned by this, some of my best friends do this most of the crucial times. They just read me, see through me just like one of those x-ray scans at the airport, they just, totally catch me before even I could start off with them.

Damn man, how do they do that, I still don't know, it's incredible, and am just blessed to have them in life. I hope they are blessed too!

Terrance: OK bro, did you see yesterday's action movie on TV?

Jayce: *Speed - Keanu Reeves* movie? Well, I get it. so it's about that scene right, isn't it?

Terrance was stunned again, and whispered to himself, "god was this guy spying over me or something, how does he know this?"; then replied - yeah, but again how did you know that I was referring to that scene.

Jayce: Will say that later, but tell me what do you think about that scene?

Terrance: That scene was confusing, I first thought the hero was trying to suffocate and kill the lady.

Jayce burst out laughing, no bro, not that!

Terrance: Why are you laughing, then what was that?

Jayce: Buddy that is called a "*smooch*" or even a "*lip lock*". It's an expression, a peaceful and loving way of telling someone that *I love you*. It's a way of expressing your feelings to someone. And girls love it seriously good, if you are a good kisser that is. Haven't you tried?

Terrance got a kick on his head, what, no I haven't, have you?

Jayce: Chuckled again, and said of course I have and you must try it too. It is the only way to complete your conversation with the girl and express your love.

Terrance: Well I don't know about that buddy, am confused, and am not able to understand this, it's dangerous, don't you think, you can even suffocate and kill a girl if not done right.

Jayce started off laughing and laughing and on.

Terrance was confused again, what the heck was that all about, was he talking sense?

So now tell me **Jayce**, how did you guess that I was referring to that scene in the first place, how did you figure it out when I mentioned only the name of the movie to you and never mentioned anything about this scene?

Jayce: Listen carefully, will tell you about that secret skill now. You see all those boys playing there, that group right there?

Terrance: Yeah, well what about them?

Jayce *trying to control his laugh*, said, you see all those boys have been asking me about that same scene that you have just asked me about, right from this morning, and am tired of explaining it. And he then burst out laughing again.

To this, even **Terrance** laughed his lungs out.

But his words were confusing him still, was **Jayce** telling the truth, was that the way to express love to a girl, did girls take that as an expression of love, won't that choke and kill her, why does someone have to do that, was that the complete way of expressing love to someone, was that legal at least?

Terrance now has a rain of thoughts.

Can a </**Kiss**> kill?

Chapter Five – Must Know Your Language

Terrance was ashamed and, in a situation, where he couldn't read his native language aloud to ten people.

It was not because he couldn't speak out loud but because he didn't know how to read his mother tongue, his native language, and this is what education lands you into at times.

The focus was always on the English language; learning to read, write, and speak English was the motto of all CBSE schools then.

It was considered a shame as per his teacher who taught him the native language. She used to embarrass him in front of other kids. But the fun part was that 38 out of 40 kids in his class were in his shoes.

One day at the language class, it was bad, and things got out of **Terrance**'s hands when his teacher started beating him while reading a story in the said language with loads of blunders.

He was pissed off at this.

And challenged his language teacher, “Just pick any story and I will read it without any mistakes tomorrow morning right in your class".

Language Teacher: Alright, is that so, then here you go. Read the story of Mahatma Gandhi tomorrow!

Terrance: (*Whispering*), Oh god, I just dug my own grave.

Language Teacher: (*With a crude expression*), take page number seven, the lesson about Mahatma Gandhi.

Terrance: Great, I will do just that for tomorrow.

On his way back home **Terrance** was wondering who Mahatma Gandhi was, and why was he in his textbook.

What did he do to become a chapter in my language textbook?

Never heard anyone say anything about him before.

Terrance was curious to know!

He reached home and surprisingly found his father there. He then looked at the clock, was it 9 pm, or was the clock wrong?

Dad: I came home early today, let's go for a movie.

Terrance: Yippee, that is awesome.

So Dad, Mom, and Sister and him on reaching the crowded theater were a bit tensed about getting the tickets as the line to the counter was long.

God, did everyone's father reach home early today?

Finally got the tickets, but **Terrance** had a doubt - which movie are we watching?

Everyone standing in the ticket line laughed at this.

His sister was eagerly looking forward to this movie and was hurrying up, hey walk faster.

Terrance: Yo stop pushing, am walking right.

Sister: I don't want to miss the first scene.

Terrance: What is there in the first scene, (*this he has heard before*), it is like people could miss the last scene of a movie but not the first scene. Why is that?

Sister: Talk less and walk more, please.

It was an animated movie and a story of a lion cub's journey to become the king of his land.
Terrance met new emotions in rainbow colors that day.

After the movie, he was disturbed.

Was that my story, is my story going to be like that, am I the lion cub in that movie?

He had thoughts raining on him!

Terrance was having a deep sleep that night, and suddenly a wave of light flashed through, there was a black shire horse, and standing next to it was a warrior face covered, heavily armed with a urumi (*an Indian sword with a flexible, whip-like blade*) secretly worn around the waist, a heater shield, and a katana on his back.

How was that technically possible, how can someone know the art of using three deadly and robust mythological weapons known to mankind?

Trrrrrrring, **Terrance** woke up with a heavy head.

What was that, oh god!

Ready for school now, he was a bit gloomy still.

He wanted to tell someone what he saw - will tell **Jayce** today.

Terrance was now in the language class.

You ready for the challenge, right?

The girl sitting next to him asked.

Terrance: What challenge?

Holy God, how can I forget that, am doomed, am dead meat today?

Language Teacher: Hey, **Vikram** read the lesson story about Mahatma Gandhi on page number seven loudly to the class, please.

Terrance was perplexed; did she tell someone else to read the story?

Has she forgotten about their challenge?

What is this confusion?

Vikram was trembling and wasn't reading the story correctly; he made a lot of mistakes while reading.

The language teacher stopped him and told **Jahnavi** to read the same lesson, she also made equal mistakes while reading it out loud to the class.

To this, the language teacher was frustrated and disappointed and left without saying anything to anyone after the class.

Terrance was also sad, for the fact that he couldn't complete the challenge, he was miserable about not being able to stand up to what he wanted to prove.

So he decided to speak to his language teacher and apologize for what he did.

He waited till the lunch break for this.

Grabbed some guts and went to the teacher's room to meet her.

Terrance: Teacher could I speak to you for a minute?

Language Teacher: Yes, please.

Terrance: I am extremely sorry for what I did. And thank you for not scolding me in class for that.

Language Teacher: Looking at your face, I understood that you haven't read the chapter and I was disappointed. Hence didn't want to take the scene further with you.

But tell me why weren't you prepared **Terrance**, don't you like this language or aren't you interested to know your grounds?

I purposely gave you that lesson to make you aware of who that person was and what his contribution was to our country, but you didn't even try, did you?

Terrance: Sorry teacher, I didn't try, I forgot about it, I seriously did, yesterday after a long time I saw my dad early at home, was excited and we went for a movie after a very long time.

Language Teacher: It's fine then, I guess this is how it is going to be for all kids, they all want to just pass the exam and go on in life, but don't want to know about their native language.

Take my word, a time will come when you would have to know your language better, I pray that you wouldn't regret then.

Terrance left school with regret that day.

He reached home and first thing, he opened that book and went up to the lesson on page seven.

He couldn't understand a thing, about the man as his ability to read the language was bad.

He was reading it, like a foreign language, which was terrible.

Terrance stopped reading, he was empty and regretted his actions.

He couldn't read the language that he spoke daily.

He was in tears - is this the end, can't I ever read my own language?

Terrance decided to narrate the entire scene to his mother.

Mother: I am glad that you realised that, you made a mistake. But how are you going to correct this?

Terrance: I don't know.

Mother: Can you reverse time?

Terrance: Not possible, I guess.

Mother: (*Laughing*), Yes you can, by letting everyone forget that time.

Terrance: How?

Mother: Learn and read that lesson in class, simple!

Happiness was back on his face, but how, I don't know to read this language well Mom.

Mother: I will read it out to you a couple of times, just listen carefully.

And she did it spontaneously, wow, it was wonderful listening to her voice.

This language was sounding more and more interesting as she read.

Terrance suddenly realized that he had seen the picture of the man on the page elsewhere.

Yes, it was on the currency note.

He then asked his mother who is this man, and why was he on my textbook.

Mother: It is because of this man that we are here all alive right now.

Terrance: Is he God?

Mother: No, but God sent. He is one reason for the freedom of our country.

Terrance knew the meaning of freedom; well, every boy knew freedom from school at least.

And he tried reading from what he heard.

Wow, that worked.

The next day he was ready to drop bombs on everyone with this.

He went with time.

The language teacher came in, and **Terrance** stood up, could I please read the lesson?

Language Teacher: Yes, go ahead.

It felt like he was rapping, 8 Mile - Eminem style.

The entire class was stunned.

Hell, he could read that language now.

Terrance went on and on until it ended in grace.

He was sounding proud; he had completed the story on the same note as his mother did. He also told the class who *Mahatma Gandhi* was and about his contribution to the country.

There was a graveyard silence after he was done, which was soon broken by the language teacher's applause - I am so proud that we have arrived in time.

There are about 6,500 languages on our planet, can someone practically learn it all?

Well, the point is, one would have to learn all if he or she has to connect with those people better.

Knowing someone's language is the key to knowing their culture, their religion, and their people.

Language has even become a criterion these days if you are looking for a job opportunity in another state or country.

Only if you know their local language would you get hired, even though English has become the universal language.

Your language has become your identity, it's your passport, it's what you are, and it speaks more about you.

So it is important to know your language first before knowing anything else.

Know yourself before knowing everything else around.

My eyes are moist while writing this, while I realize that am not writing this in my native but the universal language known to mankind, maybe I will soon after this manuscript is made into a book of sense and after an acknowledgment. That will be a tribute to my teacher and my friends in this lifetime.

So do you, know your <**Language**/>?

Chapter Six – *Friend*s Never Leave Your *Ship*

Terrance's life was running smoothly, he became a hero the other day at school, his friends were for him, his teachers admired him, his parents loved him to bits and his sister?

His school was the best place on planet Earth after home.

His neighborhood was flooded with his relatives and school friends.

The game of cricket was pacing into all alive. It was a common game and the easiest to be played without a huge ground. Even a tree or lamp post could be made as wickets to play.

The neighborhood had kids from other schools as well, and there were serious cricket match competitions happening.

It was a win-win situation for the kids from **Terrance**'s school.

Whenever their country won a match the kids used to imitate the same the next day.

Most of the matches were against his school and at times they lost miserably to their favorite foe the Greese Academy.

I have heard people say, that cricket is the easiest game in this World.

Well, could be for the people who haven't played it. But for the people who have played, it's more than just a game!

The game was happening on and off, one day at school, his best friend **Jayce** came up to him with a bomb.

Jayce: Buddy!

Terrance: Wassup!

Jayce: I am leaving school.

Terrance was frozen, his face was painted with grey and blue - sadness crept into his life again in a flash. He didn't understand what was happening to his mind.

Jayce seeing his face got worried - snap out buddy, hey, you okay?

Terrance: You are also going for good?

Jayce: Bro am just leaving school man, not our friendship, I was there for you, and will always be there for you no matter what.

Terrance: (*Still in grey*) Wish you good luck in your journey ahead, god be with you.

Jayce: Hey chillax man, don't be sad and all.

Terrance: What else should I be? First **Lilly** left and now you!

Jayce: Buddy, you forgot about the school telephone directory?

Terrance: What about it?

Jayce: You fool, it has my phone number and we will be in touch for sure - right?

Terrance: Oh yeah, right, that's awesome.

Jayce: Let's talk on all Saturdays.

Terrance: That will be good, but are you sure that would happen?

Jayce: Why not bro, and don't forget our code “Senshi nei, noi Toki wai nai 3".

Terrance: (*sighed*), Buddy, I feel like I a, stuck in time like *Jonny Quest* when you said that you were leaving school. But am hoping that you still stay in my ship called *friendship*.

Jayce: (*Burst out laughing*), that's my ship too!

It's painful when friends leave and the only happiness that you are left with is the fact that they are still alive. Some leave and some come in. Some keep in touch and some can't.

Why do you always wait?

Don't wait till you miss them forever,
Don't wait for their news,
Everybody is busy in their own Wonderland,
Don't wait till you see them next,
Don't wait till you find them next,
Don't wait as the wait won't wait for you always,
Don't wait till your Ship sinks!

So, do you have a </missing> [**Ship**\]?

Chapter Seven – A Trip On Trance

Summer holidays began.

Wow, no school for another three months.

Terrance was overloaded with happiness.

He was planning a series of events just like the other kids in his neighborhood, every kid had a lucrative plan for the next three months.

Then he over heard, his dad telling mom, “I am off for three weeks from work for the family trip”.

Huh, what family trip was he talking about?

He had no clue.

Soon the news was out at their dining table: “okay, folks we are going for a trip, starting this Friday, his dad announced”.

Horaay, **Terrance** was thrilled, but eh! Where are we going?

Dad: To *Sanctum Mare*, the most enthralling spot in the world.

And suddenly **Terrance** felt like he got a bullet shot on his head.

Terrance: But Dad, why? Not again; we have been there at least five times since...

Dad: No questions please. This place is perfect for a family holiday, it has a beautiful beach, the food is out of the world and the main attraction is the famous holy shrine. Moreover, it is the ideal destination for a pack of 10 families.

Terrance: *Whaaaaat* I thought it was just us, who in the world are those 10 families? Please tell me that it's not your relatives, Dad?

Dad: (*Chuckles*) Who else could it be? And by the way, correction, it's “our relatives”.

Terrance's plans were all just washed away by a wave of disappointment.

He was Black-Red and didn't have a choice but to go.

It wasn't because he never liked his dad's relatives, but that destination was a frequent visit, hence, it will be boring to go there again.

Who doesn't like exploring, would you visit the same place more than thrice?

Maybe other than your favorite restaurant or workplace (*lol*).

Home is an exception, *please*!

It's like dating and breaking up with the same girl *thrice*. God, who does that? Huh, Did you?

So **Terrance** thought he could ditch this trip on a vote, and tried convincing his sister, luck wasn't even close.

It was that Thursday evening, a day before the trip.

Terrance was at the family lunch, with that pack of 10 families (*Dad's relatives*).

Oh wait, it was only 9, with one missing, who could that be?

Was the count wrong?

Anyways, it indeed was a joyful gathering, there was a sumptuous gastronomic spread on the table.

The climate changed with the aroma and had a mix of flavors from various South Indian cuisines known to mankind.
Just like any hungry foodie, **Terrance** was cemented; he didn't know where to start and what to eat first.

It was a battle between his taste buds (*tongue*) and stomach, as to who will get to relish first.

And suddenly, the scene changed.

Terrance saw that black horse and that warrior standing in the middle of the same desert.

Swoooooosh - Water splashes on the his face, where did the water come from in the middle of a desert.

Sister: (*Yelling*) Wake up, you lazy log, we are leaving in an hour, dress up don't be late!

Damn, it was that dark dream again, why am I seeing this, what is that all about?

Terrance had already packed his bag last night, it was 4 am and dark, he had a heavy head and was quite drowsy.

Mam, let me freshen up before I see the next dream.

Terrance got out and saw a big blue caravan bus, right in front of his house.

Gosh, everyone was hurrying in as if the bus was going to take off from the ground like in *Harry Potter* any minute now.

How can people be awake and excited at 4 am, that too for this boring trip?

He was the last one to board the bus, hence got the convertible seat behind the driver. This was the best spot to be away from the rest of the crowd, **Terrance** was hence a bit happy.

The drive began.

One of the best parts of any trip from home is when you know for sure that there is a return journey, and that feeling is ineffable.
Never start a trip if you don't have a place to come back to.

A trip is not to forget the past nor present, but to make the future and to re-write the past.

Never start a trip to run away from things as it will find you somewhere.

Never start a trip to leave someone as you will lose yourself.

Always start a trip to give yourself a kickstart. As in this trip, “You” are going to find the better “You”.

And if you have that someone special waiting behind. Just trust in yourself.

You will encounter the trance of life soon.

Have you ever driven through the god's own country?

Well, you must do that and then read what I have written below again to get the right feel and understand it better!

Terrance was sleepy, it was 5 am. But he couldn't sleep as the bus was noisy.

He had a blurred vision of things around, he was fighting sleep.

The bus halted between the trip, he didn't know why nor where he was.

Drowsiness makes your sight foggy.

Most of them got out of the bus for some fresh air.

Terrance was disinterested in even lifting his head.

That's when he heard someone yelling "chai chai" (*tea*).

The aroma was too good; he could sense the energy in it, and his soul wanted tea, but his body wasn't willing.

God, drowsiness was a killjoy.

With his mind playing the fool, **Terrance** was now craving a cup of tea.

He couldn't deal with this anymore, so he got up and crash, someone fell in front of him.

There was a loud yell, a girl just flew off her feet.

Damn, he did it this time, an invitation to big trouble again.

Terrance: Rising to the situation, are you okay?

His eyes popped and froze; it felt like he had just crashed his car in the Formula One Grand Prix. He accidentally head-butted, **Neenu** down, just like *Zinedine Zidane* did in the World Cup.

Oh no, it was her again, and her's was the 10th family on this trip; the bus had halted for them.

What a way to meet a girl.

And now she had a bruise on her brown cheek.

Terrance was about to apologize to **Neenu** and that's when an aunt of his came rushing into this scene and took her away.

Oh, don't worry, it's gonna be fine, it's just a small bruise and no broken bones, she said.

Terrance couldn't spit more words to this mess. He was in stealth mode, now he couldn't get a tea nor speak to **Neenu** and apologize.

Neenu was staring at him in anguish, it was intense.

She looked at him like a saw-scaled viper behind a bush, ready to strike.

But this was from the girl's point of view.

Terrance noticed that her eyes were red.

Was she crying all this time?

Or was she drowsy?

She had dark blue pupils, which I guess was because of the same colored glass windows on the bus.

Her short, black, pulchritudinous (*this a better word than beautiful*) hair was tempting to hold on to. Her dark mocha brown teasing lips couldn't be described more in any language I know of. She had *Barbie*-like eyebrows. Her nose was a delicate masterpiece—softly sculpted, with a gentle curve that seemed designed for stolen kisses. It crinkled slightly when she laughed, a little wide quirk that made her all the more irresistible. Her faintest blush, like a flower, dusted my heart cold. And when she tilted her head, the golden sunlight traced its elegant slope, making it seem as if the very air adored her as much as I did. She looked like a beautiful ancient goddess—ethereal, timeless, and untouchable, as if the very air around her had been woven from golden light.

There was a quiet power in the way she carried herself, a grace that made the world seem slower, as if even time itself hesitated in her presence.

KRA-KA-THOOM

Terrance got hit by a thunderbolt. Ripping his mind and heart in bits.

Sudden, electrifying, and utterly inescapable. It crashed through his heart with a blinding flash, setting every nerve ablaze with her presence. His breath caught in his throat, the world around him fading into a distant rumble, drowned out by the storm she had ignited within him.

In that instant, he knew—there was no shelter from thunderbolts like this. It didn't whisper or warn. It hits fast, fierce, and maybe forever.

It wasn't just attraction. It was the kind of emotion that **burned**—that left his skin tingling, his mind lost in her gravity. She was the thunderbolt, bright and untamed.

No shelter, no escape from the rain of thoughts, and only the undeniable truth that **Terrance** had become a boat without a sail in the storm she had become in his life.

And in that second again, there were these echoes of thunderbolts rumbling through his soul, he knew... he would never be the same; hence had to just let himself sail in her storm.

The weight of it all pressed into **Terrance**'s chest, a silent storm swelling inside him—too heavy to shake, too deep to name. His body felt weak, maybe from exhaustion, maybe from something heavier—something that had nothing to do with sleep and everything to do with **Neenu**.

In reality, **Terrance** wasn't just tired.

He was syncing with the trance of life, drifting somewhere between memory and longing, caught in the storm she had left behind.

"*God, wish I could talk to her, just once. Just to tell her what I felt while I sailed with her*."

The thought clung to him like mist on the ocean, lingering, refusing to fade. That day—their day—felt like a lifetime ago, and yet, it pulsed through **Terrance** as if it had just happened.

And the cruelest part?

Neenu would never know.

She would never understand the way her presence had shaken him, the way her thunderbolt had struck his soul, splitting him open with its raw, electric force.

She had been the storm—wild, unrelenting, and impossible to escape—while he was the boat, trembling beneath her touch, set ablaze by the fire she never even knew she struck.

Even now, it was still raining thoughts.

A quiet, unrelenting downpour of memories, of unspoken words, of a feeling that had never been given the chance to take root.

Yet, in his heart, **Terrance** was still on that trip with her—sailing through the past, caught in the currents of what could have been.

And it's still raining thoughts!

Terrance was on this trip with her.

So, are you ready for this <**Trip**/>?

Chapter Eight – Rain, Horn, And A Desert

Apologize not just when you know that you are wrong, but also when you know that the person at the other end is badly hurt.

Ensure that you never repeat it, and assure that person that you didn't mean to hurt; it is also a crime to hurt anyone verbally. I think that's worse than physically hurting someone.

You have no idea what the other person would have gone through because of your action, the impact can cause deep emotional injuries that can't be easily repairable.

Never hurt your kid - they are just building their stories, don't break them into bits.

Never hurt your parents - they gave their everything to you and pushed you so far.

Never hurt your friends - they were there at all points of your life's turmoil and never gave up on you.

Never hurt your siblings - they only have you in this world after your parents are gone.

And most importantly, never hurt your colleagues - they are only there for a specific purpose as you are, and have a lot happening in their lives as well.

Do you have a problem with someone?

Just speak out, listen, understand, appreciate, and resolve - that's what my best friend **Sanjay** says all the time I screw up!

Let's not wage war with others but wage war with those demons in you.

Rather than fighting with someone, first fight with yourself; *explore*, *experience*, and *expand* yourself.

The only investment that gives you assured returns every time is when you invest in yourself; and I know that for sure, at least by now you would have realized that?

Haven't you?

Terrance couldn't sleep, was pretty irritated.

He just wanted to apologize to **Neenu** and clear the air.

Why are girls extra difficult at times?

I am sure she had a reason for it, but he couldn't forget the trance that he experienced; it was inevitable, frustrating, bad, painful, regretful, and eventful.

Could she be thinking about me this time?

Let me try again. And **Terrance** instantly fell asleep.

The warrior was staring at him in the middle of this desert.

Oh, where is that black horse?

Wake up, you lazy bag, his sister was *shouting her lungs out*.

Terrance: Hey, what's wrong? Leave me alone!

Sister: You dumb fool, we are leaving for sightseeing in the next 7 minutes.

Terrance: What where am I? Where is the black horse?

Sister: It is waiting outside our hotel.

Terrance: Seriously?

Sister: Are you sick? There is no horse nor donkey, you fool. Only the bus is waiting outside, *din't you get the joke*? Am going, come down in 5 minutes else we are leaving without you.

Terrance: Hey, between, where are we now?

Sister: To Egypt!

Terrance: Joke, right?

Sister: Oh, God, you silly, we are already in the paradise of your dreams.

Terrance: *Flabbergasted*!

That day, luckily most of them were late, where is she?

Has she gone back because of me?

Am I that bad?

I don't think so!

The bus was waiting for his relatives, and the others already in the bus were waiting to grab some heavy breakfast.

But **Terrance** was waiting for her, nor was he hungry nor was he able to digest time.

Chuckles!

Great, seems like **Neenu** was as lazy as I am or maybe she was getting ready.

Girls at that phase are time poisonous.

Speak of the devil, and there she was, *thudd*.

Did she break the bus door?

Was she still angry?

Terrance wanted to greet **Neenu**, but she didn't even glimpse at him.

God, do I exist?

Neenu just went through me. Man, am I *Casper*?

Her eyes were still dull; was she okay?

Whenever you want to reach your destination faster, it seems like the miles are getting longer. I still don't know why I have always felt that my place of work is near to home and never the other way around. Every time I take a long break and head home, I feel like the miles are always getting longer. Have you felt the same?

What if the milestones showed longer in your journey?

It's a sign that you are on the right path.
Congratulations!

And it's gonna teach you more than it would have in a shorter route to the same destination. So stay calm when you see the storm, stay calm when you see the earth cracking, stay calm when you see floods. You are arriving soon.

Terrance was irritated.

Come what may, I am going to speak to her today.

The bus suddenly halted, and everyone just rushed out for lunch.

Where is this place, is lunch given for free, why is everyone rushing?

Neenu's Dad - It's the best restaurant in this paradise.
Terrance - (*Mumbling*), Seems like he found this restaurant, what a jerk!

Neenu's Dad - Did you say something?

Terrance - Oh, uncle, I was trying to figure out what to eat.

Neenu's Dad - (*Diving in*), I will help you with that. And started reading out the menu, describing in depth the history of the dishes on the food menu.

Terrance regretted what he just said as he went on for almost an hour.

Neenu: *Father*, I guess you should decide a dish for him rather.

Neenu's Dad - Oh, yes, you are right. *Waiter*, please get a portion of deep-fried fish and ghee rice.

Terrance - Thank you, uncle, for the kindness!

Neenu: Sorry about that, he gets excited at times.

Man, was **Neenu** alright?

Was it some kind of mood swing or split personality?

Terrance was a bit wordless to this, and she was about to leave.

Terrance: Not at all, uncle was just helping me to read the menu!

Neenu: (*Howled out laughing*).

And she wasn't stopping it. Gosh, is she mental?

That's when **Terrance** could feel that **Neenu** was drawing attention around, and he decided to slip out of the situation.

Neenu: Hey, where do you think you are going? Don't you wanna talk to me?

Terrance: (*stupefied*). How does she do that? Damn, I know that she was in my head, but could she hear me? Impossible!

Neenu: You, alright?

Terrance: How did you know that I wanted to speak to you?

Neenu: (*Giggles*) The fairy godmother told me!

Terrance: Fairy? I have heard this somewhere before, 1st grade at school, right?

Neenu: Wait, you haven't met the fairy godmother?

Terrance: Oh, does she live close by?

Neenu: (*Fighting laughter*), you are so funny and real. Then *laughed* and *laughed* like a hyena.

Terrance, waiting for **Neenu** to finish laughing, and said I think I like you!

What did I just do?

Why, oh, god?

What did I just say?

Neenu: Oh, well, I think I have a soft corner for you now.

Terrance: Really! But why only now? Why not before?

Neenu: You have a bad memory, or else you are trying to trick me.

Terrance: No ways, why should I?

Neenu: All boys do that.

Terrance: I didn't understand.

Neenu: You are still a kid and won't understand.

Terrance: Have heard that before!

Neenu: How could you forget? You kicked me at the festival event purposely when we met for the first time and again head-butted me down yesterday. You did all that to talk to me, right?

Terrance: What, are you serious? No, no ways, it was an accident, and I am extremely sorry. I wanted to apologize to you instantly. But you walked away pissed, I guess.

Neenu: No, in fact, I wanted to talk to you then and even now, but...

She was the most amazing trance **Terrance** went through until now. She knew that **Terrance** had something more than "*like*" for her.

Seeing her dark blue eyes, **Terrance** was feeling light, her face was arresting his time. How could she have done that?

She was like *Professor X* from X-Men, who could stop time in the non-technical sense. She created a "pause" effect in **Terrance**'s mind and locked his memory in that specific period.

KRA-KA-THOOM

Thunderbolts struck him again, a black charcoal color background filled the sky, tickling cool breeze flew into the scene with rain picking pace.

Everyone ran into the bus, but **Terrance** was stuck.

Soaked he was in her rain of thoughts.

Wow, coincidence, I can't resist saying that, it's raining right now as I write.

Hope it rains while you are reading, too!

Horn hornnnn, that was the loudest sound **Terrance** had ever heard till then.

The driver was screaming, “Yo, hey, move away, boy, and get in; everyone is waiting to leave”.

That's when he realized that he was standing right in front of the bus.

That day's sightseeing trip was forgotten, as **Terrance** had discovered a sight of something extraordinary, a sight of illusion that even I am finding difficult to express in words. Hope you see it.

Neenu was a mirage in **Terrance**'s deserted soul.

So, is it </**Raining**>? And did you hear that <**Horn**>?

Chapter Nine – *Mom*, Sorry I Accidentally Kissed A Girl and Am *Thalassophobic*

As per the itinerary, the next day had a visit to the holy place.

Terrance's seat on the bus was occupied.

Where am I gonna sit now?

Quickly, happiness sprouted on his face.

Neenu had reserved a seat next to her.

Terrance felt that he had rollerskates on. Wait, am I walking or skating towards her?

God, why me?

This trip might change my life.

He was super tongue-tied.

Neenu: (*Whispering*) I thought you wanted to sit next to me?

Terrance: (*Super shocked*!)

Neenu: (*Giggles*)

The bus trip was hard and bumpy.

There was a graveyard silence on the bus.

I guess it was the heavy breakfast.

Most of them were snoring, huh, how can someone doze off in this bumpy ride?

Neenu too?

That's okay; let her sleep for a while.

The bus took a sharp U-turn and *kiss*!

Terrance got kissed on his cheek.

God, what was that?

Did I get bitten by a *snake*?

Huh, **Neenu** was still sleeping.

But now, resting her head on **Terrance**'s shoulder and slid down in a cuddle.

Now her face was almost pressed on his chest.

Terrance turned into a cotton candy instantly when he realized that his mom was watching.

Should I wake her up?

I wish I could, my heart was against that.

But my head was yelling at me to wake her up.

He felt perplexed, so pretended to sleep.

That was the best solution to this.

There was a sudden break; for a split second, **Terrance** thought that his soul had flown out of the window.
The driver had just avoided an accident, phew!

Why aren't there any seatbelts on this bus?

Wait, did I?

Terrance felt like something extremely supple had pecked his cheek.

Did she just kiss me again on my cheek?

Neenu was still fast asleep - no way, she was sleeping!

Sometime later, the bus halted.

Terrance looked out and saw a fantabulous beach facing a hotel.

This trip was already full of surprises.

Wow, is paradise the next stop?

Sister: Hey, did you get your baggage?

Terrance: Baggage! No, why?

Sister: (*Yelling*), you dumb-ass did you leave it behind at the hotel?

Terrance: Like, duhh, obviously!

Sister: You fool; we have just changed the hotel. We are gonna stay here from today.

Terrance: (*Stunned*) Darn, I didn't know that, and no one said anything about this change.

Their **Mom** came into this conversation - Don't worry, I have brought your bag, **Terrance**.

Since you were busy, I couldn't let you know, and *chuckles*.

Terrance: *Phew*, that was close. Thank you, **Mom**, for the help, as always!

Wait, why did she chuckle after saying that?

God, she knows what I am up to!

A mother knows what is best for her child, she can be the best critic.

If she can bring you to this world by tearing herself open.

Then I am sure that she can even see through you, just like she could when you were in her womb.

She could sense your movement, so I am sure she could feel you even now.

I am a true victim of that.

My mother could sense me coming home, and before I rang that doorbell, she would open it.

Even when I am miles away, she could sense when I am sad, happy, drunk, hungry, confused, depressed, and even unwell.

There were some stunning times when I got calls from her the same second I was thinking about her.

Through my mother, I have learned a rainbow of emotions.

From her, I know how a girl feels and what a girl has gone through in life.

My mother has inspired me to reach where ever and be whatever I am right now.

She has kick-started my life, so she has all the authority to kick me when I am wrong.

And it is through her that I have first seen this world, learned to love and to be kind.

She has taught me to forgive, but never to forget.

She blushes whenever I thank her, but I know for sure that she doesn't wait to hear that.

I know being a Mother is a thankless job!

And it is from her that I have learned to seed happiness in others' dreams.

It is from her that I understood that there is this eternal power in this universe called god, who will do anything in his/her power to help you achieve something that you are chasing with your full force.

She is the one who taught me to follow peace in life. And that vengeance is only for Batman and not my weapon!

She is the one who sent me money on my birthday when my back account hardly had few zeros. I damn, don't know how she knew that my account was almost zero.

I wish I could be a better son.

I wish I could tell her that every time I left her behind on a trip back to my destination, I left with a broken heart and overflowing eyes.

I would wrestle with myself and lie to her that I would come back soon for her, but I know that she knew the fact that I was just promising for her happiness.

And I would work overtime to kill that feeling of missing her.

God give me another chance, I wish I could be born to her the next time too.

Terrance had a sumptuous gastronomic dinner!

The spread had all the authentic seafood dishes of South India.

A memorable day it was, but there was a question in his mind.

It was bothering him badly.

Then came the last surprise for the day.

Okay, kids, you all will be sleeping in the dormitory today; an aunt of his declared.

She was the best aunt in the world, God bless!

Terrance was thrilled but didn't show it out.

He wanted to be less noticed then.

The dormitory room was placed parallel to the beach.

The sound of the waves could be counted from that proximity.

And with the breeze together, it made a relaxing raga!

It was a no moon night; the sky was pitch black.

There were no beds but high-density thick mattresses to sleep on the floor; that is what happens when you visit any happening place during its peak season.

The dormitory was too small, it would have been difficult to step a foot if one more kid was sleeping there.

Terrance was in a hurry to find a spot to sleep and again smile was his best friend.

With **Neenu** around, the smile had become a shadow to him.

His opportunity to smile was too often now.

There she was, waiting just like she did on the bus.

Neenu had reserved a spot next to her for him to sleep.

Should I take it?

Will that be right?

Oh god, you there!

Neenu: Hey, what is the problem? You ok?

Terrance: (*Perplexed*), Nothing, I am good!

Neenu: I have reserved this spot for you, and guess what?

Terrance: What?

Neenu: This is the best view to the beach.

Terrance: Wow, it's wonderful.

Neenu: Seems like you didn't like it?

Terrance: No, it's just that I get a gloomy feeling when I see the beach for more than 7 minutes.

Neenu: Are you thalassophobic?

Terrance: *Thala*, what?

Neenu: Oh, ignore that. Come on; it's way past bedtime.

Okay, kids, lights off and to bed right now, his best aunt commanded.

The mattresses were like a collage on the floor because of space constraints.

Woh, now I know what a sub feels like.

Terrance slept facing **Neenu**.

Neenu: I have a secret to share.

Terrance: What's that?

Neenu: I can only say it in your ears.

Terrance: Sure, why not!

Mwah (*giggles*), then *Mmwah Smmhh Mmwah.*

Neenu kissed him again on his cheeks.

For a fraction of a second, **Terrance** was frozen like a snowman, but he immediately discovered something.

Terrance: (*Calmly*) Can I ask you something?

Neenu: Yeah! (*with wide, beetle-like eyes, with a killing stare*)

Terrance: The second kiss you gave me on the bus was deliberate, right?

Neenu: (*smiles*); even the first kiss was!

Terrance: So now I have a secret to keep forever.
Neenu: What?

Terrance: Can you come closer and look into my face?

They were surrounded by pitch-black darkness. He searched through her short hair and got a grip on her head. Guess she would have closed her eyes, but he could hear **Neenu** breathing deeply; she was also shivering slowly at times. **Terrance** then searched for her dark mocha brown lips and made her breathless for a second.

Neenu didn't want this to end soon; hence pressed him further.

Terrance felt a bolt of shivering, electrifying waves going through him.

What was she feeling?

Was it the same?

He suddenly saw a torch light pass and snapped out of this scene.

Terrance: (*Shaken*), Are you okay?

Neenu: (*Whispering*), What happened? Keep your voice low.

Terrance: I am so sorry. I didn't mean to do that. I saw that in a movie and...

Neenu: (*Holding him close softly and calming him down*), (*stil whispering*), It's okay I am fine, relax, even I wanted to try it someday.

Terrance: You did. Oh, but for a sec, I thought you couldn’t breathe; did I suffocate you?

Neenu: Really? Let me check. Just come closer again, here!

And their movie continued for another second and stopped; both of them were in a trance of what was happening.

Was it right or wrong?

And then again they tapped out of this trance, couldn't speak to each other.

They felt weird and slept away from each other.
Terrance felt a little locked.

Oh, god, what did I just do?

Was someone watching all this?

He was shit scared to open his eyes and slept off unknowingly.

Terrance could only hear the beach and the breeze for now and doesn't even remember who dozed off first nor how many times they kissed.

He was back in a trance by her kiss.

He felt frozen at times, but what he will never forget is the first kiss; a kiss of confusions.

A kiss he wanted to explore again.

A kiss of happenings.

A kiss that took him somewhere and brought him back to somewhere else.

His head had **Neenu** doing a ballet, he couldn't feel anything as was Numb like that *Linkin Park* Song.

So, are you ready to meet that <**Confusion**>?

Chapter Ten – Only "That Someone" Can Break Your Time

Terrance reached home after school. Was feeling delighted, it was a Friday.

His Dad, Mother, and Sister were waiting for him.

Come, let's leave, Dad said.

Terrance: (*Clapping*), Another movie?

Dad: No, we are going to my cousin's house.

Great, seems like it could be another gastronomical dinner.

Would she be there? he *wondered*.

On reaching, many unknown faces were visiting and returning from the house chanting prayers.

But a few people around **Terrance** were weeping.

Neenu was sitting on the floor with her face covered.

Her mom and two sisters looked shattered and drained.

Terrance could sense grief and sadness around, his mother's eyes were moist.

Later a priest arrived and a coffin was brought into the scene.

Terrance: What is happening, why is...

Sister: (*Hush*), Keep quiet, please.

Terrance: Ok alright, but can't you tell me what's happening?

And there was a sudden screech.

They had opened the coffin and there he was resting in peace, it was **Neenu**'s father.

Am I carrying a horse on my back?

What was that smell?

Terrance was perplexed.

And then he saw his cousin granny **Karmila**. She was a teacher to all in his family and the neighbourhood.

Granny, what is happening?

Why am I feeling weird watching all this?

Karmila: You are feeling weird because there is kindness in you.

You are surrounded by the smell of a soul departing. This assures us, uncle is on his way to meet god today. He will be traveling through the seven worlds to eternal peace at God's paradise. One more thing constant in this world is death. It could be delayed, but cannot be stopped. Next could be me and one day you, she said in the most ethereal and seraphic voice ever heard.

Time has blocked my way, I can't reach you.

Terrance stood there watching everyone else abandon in the flow of time.

What can I tell you and how can I console you.

The loss is yours, only you will know the pain and only you will know the gap in time.

But God will heal you, he is with you now and only he can lift you back.

This is what my granny told me, and this is what **Terrance** wanted to tell **Neenu**.

But I am mute today, my heart gave up on me, my legs aren't for me, my hands have cheated me today.

Thought, I am a strong warrior who has battled all seasons in life.

But you are raining on me.

If I close my eyes, it might stop raining!

I don't want that, I can't do that. Will I see you again, **Neenu**?

I spoke a million words you couldn’t hear; only the other me in me knows what I said that day. I wanted to hold you tight and not let go.

I tried a billion times to speak to the shattered you, but...

Son, it's time for us to leave, his Dad said.

Terrance couldn't look back as it was history.

He sank in time and could see time sprinting away from him like *Usain Bolt.*

There is no way you can catch up with time; it's always ahead.

Time heals, but it will still remind you of the past.

When you lose someone, is when you know, that someone wasn't just another someone to you; and that someone was a lot more than a normal someone for you and more than someone else.

And that someone had left changing your time for maybe someone else to enter your life.

So go with my prayers and hope that someone is coming into your life soon!

Stop not to search, as what you search has been searching for you since and is just a search away...

So, will you stop </**Searching**>?

Thank You, "____________"

This I really can't express in words.

Thank you for reading it to the end. That means more to me than you know.

Writing this book was like reliving every thunderbolt that shaped me—some painful, some beautiful, all unforgettable. But what truly matters is that you were here for the journey.

From the first page to the last, you became a part of this story, and for that, I'm beyond grateful.

Life has a way of teaching us through unexpected moments, and if even one lesson from these pages resonated with you, made you reflect, or gave you a new perspective, then this book has done its job.

Thank you for your time, your curiosity, and your willingness to dive into this journey with me.

You are officially part of my story now, and I hope, in some small way, this book has become a part of yours too.

Until we cross paths again—whether in another book, another story, or just in the shared experiences of life—keep chasing the lessons, embracing the thunderbolts, and writing your own incredible journey.

With Love & Thunderbolts,

Tony Storm

This is just the beginning - stay tuned for *Part 2*.

If this book spoke to you, leave a review and share it with a friend who might need it, too!

From My Rain Of Thoughts

Let my Hope be with you in tough times!

Published By Tony Storm

This book is a work of fiction, blending self-help, romcom, and nostalgia-driven storytelling. While inspired by real emotions and experiences, all characters, events, and dialogues are purely fictional. Any resemblance to actual persons, living or dead, is purely coincidental.

The lessons and insights shared in this book are based on personal interpretations and experiences. They are meant for reflection, inspiration, and entertainment, not as professional advice. Readers are encouraged to apply their own judgment and seek guidance from qualified professionals when making important life decisions.

The author is not responsible for any interpretations, feelings, or personal experiences that may relate to the content of this book. Any connections drawn are purely individual and unintentional.

Thank you for respecting the creative work that went into this book.

www.ingramcontent.com/pod-product-compliance
Ingram Content Group UK Ltd.
Pitfield, Milton Keynes, MK11 3LW, UK
UKHW041317190726
13845UKWH00025B/343

9 789334 269703